My Shadow

by Robert Louis Stevenson

illustrated by Sara Sanchez

Sky Pony Press
New York

I have a little shadow
that goes **in** and **out** with me,

And what can be the use of him
is more than I can see.

He is very, very like me

from the heels

up to the head;

And I see him **jump** before me,

when I jump
into my bed.

The funniest thing about him
is the way he likes to grow.

Not at all like
proper children,
which is always very
slow;

For he sometimes shoots up

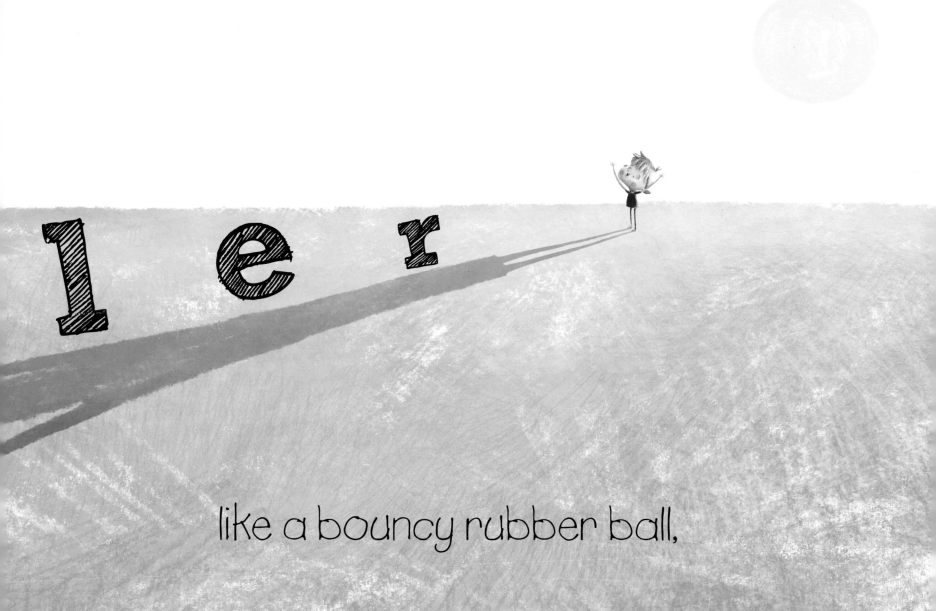

l e r

like a bouncy rubber ball,

And he sometimes gets so little
that there's none of him at all.

He hasn't got a notion of how
children ought to play,

And can only make a fool of me
in every sort of way.

He stays so close beside me,

he's a **coward**, you can see;

I'm too brave to stick to mommy as that shadow **sticks** to me!

One morning, very early,
before the sun was up,

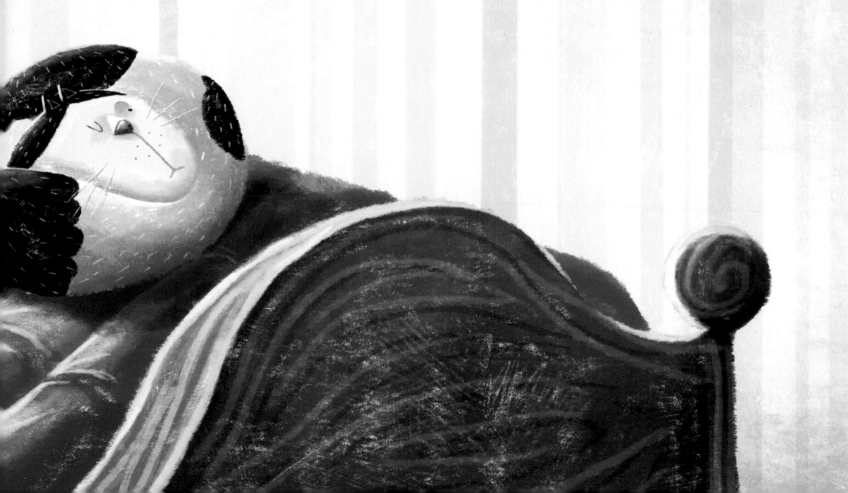

I rose and found the shining dew
on every buttercup;

But my lazy
little shadow,
like a naughty
sleepy-head,

Had stayed at home behind me
and was fast asleep in bed.

The End